I Am

J SIBI

ISBN: 1-9994539-0-9
ISBN-13: 978-1-9994539-0-9

MountainLion Publications
contact@mlionpublications.ca

Dedicated To

Appa, Amma, Nit, Hero & Rani

CONTENTS

Ice-cream

I started frozen and cold

Stuffed in a box, shaken and stirred

I was there with the others,

Some yellow, pink and brown

And others with nuts of different flavours

Occasionally the lid would open,

Flooding the box with light and warmth

Ice screamed ... 'me me me', but it was in vain

As the shiny metal hand chose my neighbour

I waited and waited till I was stiff and stone cold

Finally, the lid did open and the giant metal hand reached down

And scooped me completely in its grasp

I felt special as I was seated in the waffle cone

And the little boy's eyes lit up with excitement

As I was handed over to him

This is where my journey ends and his happiness begins

River

I watched the glacier sweat in the warmth of the
sunlight

And watched as the tiny droplets merged into one tiny
string of water

The breadth of a human hair

They were joined by many others as they formed a
watery ribbon

Carving scars down the glacier's face as they journeyed
downwards

They hit the icy bottom and continued to slide

Gently but forcefully tugged by an invisible force

Towards the distant and mighty ocean

Each ribbon merged with the other to form a stream so
wide

That it could be crossed by a walking mountain goat

The stream tricked onwards, with its waters as clear as

An innocent child's heart

Until it meets its brothers who all decided to join hands

And rumble and thunder down the mountain sides

Growing stronger and angrier at each turn

Now, there was no boulder that could stop them

Nor any tree that would not bend before their might

Villages and cities thrived on their banks

As did the fishes & crocodiles within them

They now moved with a silent grace

As they heard the welcoming oceanic waves

They rushed towards the open arms of the ocean as

A lost child returning home

For now, there is nowhere to go.

Language of silence

I travelled to places, far and wide

From icy mountains to salty oceans

In search of the answer

I asked the learned men with grey beards and bald heads

They replied in flowery words and elegant sentences

But none would answer the question

'What language does silence speak'?

Tired and penniless, I made my way

To the sun-baked land of ancient wisdom

There I found him who told everything but said nothing

For that is the language of silence

Book

I was stamped, folded and stuffed in a box

With many others who had similar stories to tell

My fate, literally, was written on my face

And my life, an open book for others to read

I was temporarily put up in a foster home

Where I saw so many like me

Some fat, some thin, some tall, some small, some
colourful, some plain

Some with a secret history and some with an
unsolvable mystery

All waiting to get into the hands of someone

Who would love and relish them

Luckily, I ended up in the hands of a little boy

Whose eyes lit up as he saw me

He enjoyed my company and

Occasionally tickled me by scribbling on me

But this was not to last as he soon grew bored

And I had other younger and colourful competitors

I now spent most of my time locked in the wooden prison

Aimlessly looking through the glass window

Time flew and I grew old and feeble, barely opening my eyes

As I contemplated the purpose of existence

I was shaken from my stupor by a pair of tiny hands

I looked into the mischievous eyes of a tiny boy

The son was now the father

I straightened my dog ears and I felt re-incarnated

Mirror

She looked longingly at me with her pretty blue eyes

Longing to be called beautiful

She caressed her golden brown locks from side to side

Changing her poise and glancing ever so slightly

From the corner of her big blue eyes

She looked again with expectant eyes

And I showed her the truth

For I don't like to play smoke and mirrors

She gasped and frowned when she saw

A tiny pimple that was threatening to erupt

Her fingers moved quickly, deftly and yet tenderly

Like a pianist's fingers caressing the keys

And the tiny volcano now lay hidden

Buried under layers of golden dust

She now looked as pretty as a blossomed flower

She came close and whispered to me

'Mirror mirror on the wall

Am I the most beautiful of them all'?

Camera

I waited earnestly with bated breath

Time seemed to crawl in the swampy grassy marshlands

The sun, tired after a long day's work

Was saying his goodbye by painting a beautiful sunset

The clouds, stained with a tinge of flamingo pink

Lay scattered in the orange sky

A lone goose flew above

Shattering the silence with its irritating cackling noise

The trees whispered their secrets

As the wind rustled through them

Shadows moved in the tall grass

And finally, my target was almost within my grasp

Shy and spotted, nimble and quick

She could escape with a bewitching grace

The deer poked her head outside the grass

As I stood still and narrowed my focus

I unleashed a flurry of unerring shots

As she was silhouetted against the golden orb

She jumped and vanished into the tall grass

But I missed none of my shots

For the pictures that I have in my heart

Will be shared with one and all

Exam

The two-hour staring contest had just begun

This silent game has some wicked rules

No talking, no eating, no weeping, no cheating

I ask him a thousand questions

He looked at me with his tired eyes

Hoping to see an oasis of compassion

In this vast desert of savage questions

But I shall show no mercy

Though he had been up all night

He scratched his head and bit his well-bitten nails

But alas, his eyes were as vacant as the mind inside

Tired, battered and with his confidence shattered

This knight retired to his dormitory

Hoping to win this battle the following semester

Snowflake

I floated gracefully and silently

Like a flower riding the gentle breeze

And twirling and twisting with excitement

The sky was not modest tonight

Cloudless and bare, she brazenly showed

The limitless glittering diamonds that she had

The lonely moon was nowhere to be seen

Perhaps, he has gone to the other side

In search of the one whom he has been searching

I looked below and saw the ground covered in white

The mountain trees stood tall on guard duty

As their residents roamed the realm of sleep

I further descended and saw a small town

Filled with colour and bright lights

Looking like the centre of a white forest cake

Christmas carols wafted through the air

And met me as I was about to touch the ground

As distinct and unique as I was

I became one with the many

White, soft, clean and spotless.

Shadow

I spring to life in the brightness

Casting a blanket of darkness where I go

Nothing escapes my grasp

Human, animal, plant or planet

I cling to them, accompanying them wherever they go

Inseparable like a Siamese twin

Trampled under innumerable boots

And run over repeatedly by buses

And yet, unscathed and unharmed

I, unflinchingly, enact their every move

I fear material objects

As a mighty lion fears the apple tree

My nemesis, the darkness, the shy and the sly one

Is hiding around the corner

Shielding her face from the bright sun

She embraced me with open arms

But I will rise and run

As soon as I see the sun

My only unfulfilled desire is

To see my own shadow.

Tree

I overhear the birds chirping

Listening to the tales of the land far beyond the dark
forest

Of the handsome prince and his beautiful princess

With eyes like blue pearls and hair like a golden river

And I yearn to see it for myself

I overhear the birds chirping

Listening to the tales of the raging river

Whose compassion was frozen in her icy cold waters

Swallowing every village and town from her banks

And I yearn to see it for myself

I overhear the birds chirping

Listening to the tales of the moving mountains

Sandy, windy, silent & empty

The home of the ship of the desert

And I yearn to see it for myself

I overhear the birds chirping

They tell tales from far & unknown lands

Of an empire's glorious history or a riveting murder
mystery

And I cuddle them, my treasured feathery friends

Who build their homes in my arms.

Pen

I wrote about the complete works of Shakespeare

And the Iliad of Homer

I cast a magical enchantment spell on all

When I wrote about the fiery dragons & half cooked
knights

I wrote about the ravages of the savage war

And sang praises about the heroes who fought in them

I contemplatively wrote about the all-pervading All
Mighty

And wrote about the argumentative and debating
atheists

I wrote about the Constitution that guarantees freedom

And the agreements that crowned dictators

I have been here since men learnt to write

And how I wish I could put a pen to paper

To write my own autobiography

But, alas, I am merely a tool

Like a chisel in the hands of a sculptor.

Rainbow

Born of the marriage of water and light

I shone brightly and in vivid colours

Like the albatross spreading its mighty wings

I stretched my ribbon like arms around the earth

Hugging her for as long as I can

I brought wonder to the faces of the people below

Cameras snapped as the air was filled with oohs and aahhhs

Excited children pointed their tiny fingers at me

As they playfully jumped over little puddles

 There are those seeking the fabled pot of gold

Alas, little do they know that they are chasing rainbows

How I wish they cherished the now

For Life has limited colourful and happy moments

I have exceeded my life expectancy, minutes after I was born

And I shall vanish into the brightness

But it was a life well lived

Bright, colourful, happy and bringing smiles to one and all

Shoes

In the beginning, I had no trouble finding my feet

And found joy in travelling around

I didn't mind the dusty streets or the wet grass

Or the crunchy sound of crushing the fallen leaves

Or the wetness of fresh snow

From the glistening floors of the dazzling shopping malls

To the dark & gloomy movie halls

I have seen them all

But now, I am so tired of being at the bottom every time

Having seen the sights and wonders of the world

I am now dead on my feet

Torn and tired, smelly and stinky

Ignored and forgotten

I wonder if it is possible for me

To commit shoecide

Television

When I am turned on

They look at me all the time

I know not why, but they look at me

All the time

While they idly sit on that old couch,

Or lie in bed, waiting for that elusive sleep

Or even in that private bathroom

Where they want to look at me

And listen to what I tell them

I know not why, but they can't stop looking at me

I can move them from joyous smiles to salty tears

From playful laughter to raging anger

From fond memories to hungry zombies

From television to tunnel vision

They look at me all the time

When I am turned on

Fall leaves

Like young birds leaving the nest

We flew away from our tree

The heartless wind, showing no mercy

As he carried us in his mighty arms

Hoping that we would be his joyful companions

On his endless journey

But, he is sure to be disappointed

Old, frail & weak

Most of us are reading the last chapter in our
storybook

Waiting to fall anytime

You can take a leaf out of our book

And live your life, bright, purposeful and colourful

When fall does come

Fly away in the wind

After saying goodbye.

Time

I have the boon of eternal life

The life of an invisible, omnipresent witness

I see things all the time

From when the monkeys came down from the trees

To the time they reached for the stars

From the birth of a helpless baby

To the spectacular death of a giant star

From the densely populated Amazon forests

To the vast empty expanse of space

I have seen it all, for I was always there

A silent observer,

With nothing to do for an eternity

I watch as things magically appear and disappear

In the cosmic fabric of the universe

And I - always have time

Tides

The battle had resumed again

My stubborn enemy and I were locked in a timeless battle

Over a few feet of barren land

And our battles were bewitched by a strange curse

The vanquisher would become the vanquished

And this time, it was my destiny to be the victor

I urged my army to rush forward

But they crept ahead at a snail's pace

Each wave, slowly but surely, covering the territory

Inch by inch

Rolling over the sand and holding on to them

For a few hours,

Until I have to withdraw

This timeless battle, between land and sea

Has seen its highs and lows

But no victor has been able to turn the tide

And claim victory once and for all.

Clouds

I stood at the crossroads of a million roads

Directions everywhere but nowhere to go

White & fluffy, featherweight & mute

I lazily hovered in the mid-air

Pondering what to do

When I was blown away by the north-westerly winds

But I didn't mind, and neither did my friends

We journeyed a thousand miles

Over farms & cities, jungles & lakes

Munching & crunching all the way

I was now dark, fat and ugly

So huge, I could block the sun

I burst into tears

Spraying torrents of water into the darkened sky

My emotional outburst left me lighter

Emotionally and physically

And I journeyed along

Floating in the sky

Sleep

I avoided him for a day

And he began losing sleep over me

His weary eyes were circled by dark clouds

Unshaven & ragged, tired & irritated

He looked like a tired traveler in search of a soft bed

A cup of freshly brewed black coffee

Couldn't jumpstart his brain

Which was operation in zombie mode

He was trapped in no man's land

Too tired to either walk to the real world

Or to slip into the dream world

I finally cast my charm over him

His half-open eyes saw nothing but darkness

As he slipped into the abyss of deep sleep.

Wig

He looked with despair at the mirror

Which only showed him what he already knew

His grabbed me with both his hands

As only I could hide his ball of shame

He ran his fingers through the hair

But that one strand of hair refused to bow down

To any fine-toothed comb

He glanced again at the truthful mirror

Round face, stubby nose, potbelly and uneven hair

Looking better but definitely worried

As his mind has spun a cocoon around itself

He needs to let his hair down

And let things straighten themselves

For the moment, he felt

Neither hair nor there.

Bubble

Round and round, I bobbled around

Bouncing meaninglessly in the air

Shrieks, screams and tiny outstretched hands

Chased me as I rushed away from them

Shiny and wearing my rainbow dress

I saw the world through my glass windows

The jumping children, the harassed parent

The sleeping grandpa and the happy toy seller

All the required ingredients for a family soup

Me and my fellow escape artists watched this spectacle

Not wasting a second, as time is of the utmost essence

Born to die, we relish and cherish each precious second

Before we pop out of our own bubble.

Web

I bounced and danced in the wind

Clutching desperately to all leaves and stems

With my silvery arms, which were radiating from my center

I was drenched in the light rain

The gentle moonlight reflecting the water droplets

Made me irresistibly beautiful to my innocent victims

He fluttered and danced towards me

And reached out to hold one of my many hands

Alas, little did he know that

He had touched the hand of Death

I held him tight and with all my might

As he twisted and turned in agony

But there was no escape

Each silvery strand bound him

In an inescapable death trap

Soon, a silver coffin was all that was visible

And I waited for my master

To enjoy his feast.